Dream Realized Books
Printed by CreateSpace, An Amazon.com Company
Copyright ©2014 by Jill Rivkin Communications

ISBN: 1500764310   ISBN-13: 978-1500764319

Crazy Hair

Written by Jill Rivkin

Illustrated by Andrea Parker

To Maya
Be confident!

Jill Rivkin

To my amazing children: Meredith and Jacob

Never could I have imagined such incredible, gorgeous, curly-haired children. You both bring light, energy, love, smarts and laughter to our home every day. And, of course, amazing curls that are as unique and as special as you are. Love you!

When I get up each morning,
there's something I always say:

"Mommy, Do I have crazy hair?
Is it curling every which way?"

Then Mommy looks at me,
with a soft smile and a giant hug.

"Sure, you have crazy hair,
but it's adorable, my little Love Bug."

It's cold outside, I need a hat.
So I bundle for the bus to school.

In the hall, I hang everything up.
Is wild hair with static electricity cool?

Off to dance, I'm a prima ballerina.
So I'll need a fancy, neat bun.

But no surprise, the curls slip right out.
My hair's a mess by the time I'm done!

When it's time to wash off the day,
we like to sing while I shower.

But sometimes my hair just makes me cry,
and when we have to comb it... I cower.

Then we curl up in bed,
thinking about the day and what tomorrow will be.

We talk about friends, how we feel, what we know,
and something becomes clear to me...

Each of us looks completely different,
no matter how crazy our hair is.

Everyone should love their curls,
their bangs, their locks, their frizz.

Some kids have spiky, straight-up hair,
and some have pig-tails in a pair.

Some kids have long, very wavy hair,
that flies around everywhere!

"Little Lady," Mommy reminds me,
"Your hair makes you different and true.

It's your own and you're simply beautiful,
from each curl – through and through."

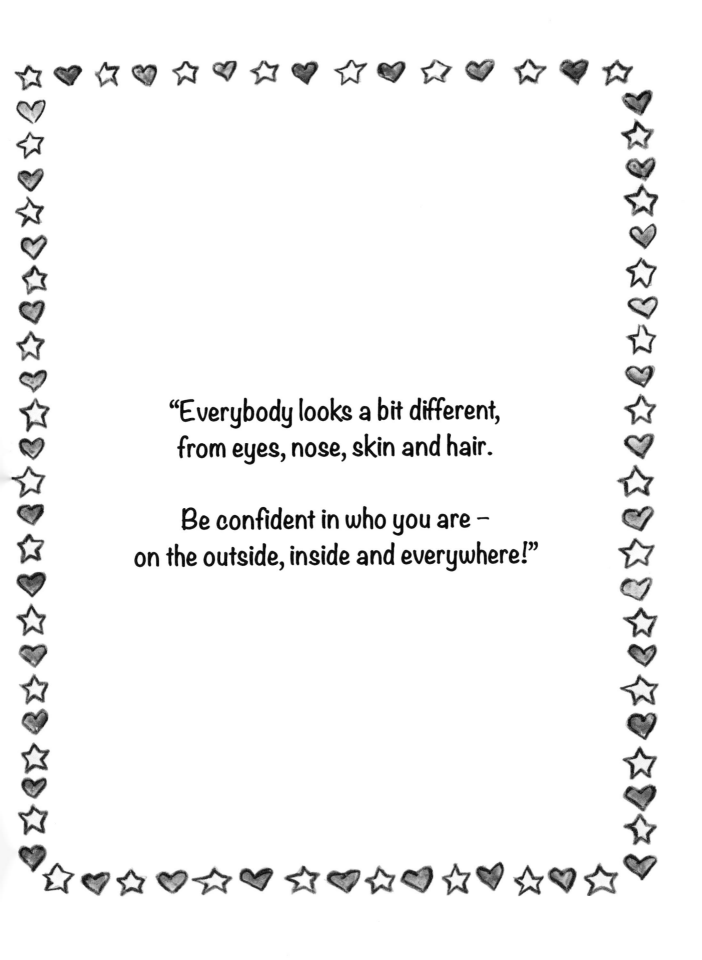

"Everybody looks a bit different,
from eyes, nose, skin and hair.

Be confident in who you are –
on the outside, inside and everywhere!"

So each day I get out of bed,
brush my teeth, and start the day.

I see my face and curls in the mirror,
and now I smile and say:

"My hair IS beautiful, Mommy.
It's special as can be.
It's not like anyone else's,
it's my own and makes me ME!"

The End